All rights reserved. Published by Scholastic Inc.
SCHOLASTIC and associated logos are trademarks and/or registered trademarks of Scholastic Inc.
ISBN 0-439-20128-4
Printed in the U.S.A.
First Scholastic printing, November 2000